T0128688

BRATLINGS

Rosalyn E. Harrington

Copyright © 2022 by Rosalyn E. Harrington. 822430

All rights reserved. No part of this book may be
reproduced or transmitted in any form or by
any means, electronic or mechanical, including
photocopying, recording, or by any information
storage and retrieval system, without permission in
writing from the copyright owner.

This is a work of fiction. Names, characters, places
and incidents either are the product of the author's
imagination or are used fictitiously, and any
resemblance to any actual persons, living or dead,
events, or locales is entirely coincidental.

To order additional copies of this book, contact:
Xlibris
844-714-8691
www.Xlibris.com
Orders@Xlibris.com

ISBN: Softcover   978-1-6698-4296-5
       Hardcover   978-1-6698-4297-2
       EBook   978-1-6698-4298-9

Print information available on the last page

Rev. date: 08/16/2022

These are stories about the mischievous ways of the nonstop antics of Mrs. Copper's third-grade class at Unity Rainbow Charter School. Here are three short stories to delight any child's imagination.

LENNY AND THE PENCIL PEN

It was a typical day at Unity Rainbow Charter School. Mrs. Copper was gathering her third class from the cafeteria after their breakfast. All the children were in line and in order, except for Lenny. "We're all waiting for you, Lenny," said Mrs. Copper.

Pointing toward the class bully Andrew, he cries, "But he hit me, and I was protecting myself."

"Lenny, we don't have time for this this morning."

"Principal Bottoms is coming to our class today for observation, and I want you to be on your best behavior. Yesterday it was Sarah who took your lunch and threw it in the trash can, only to find that it was under your desk the whole time. If this keeps up, I'm going to have to call your mother."

Poor Lenny, he didn't know what to do. He certainly didn't want Mrs. Copper to call his parents. Lenny felt so frustrated about Mrs. Copper not believing. The only thing he could do was to take out one of his colorful pencil pens and break it into tiny little pieces.

"Why do you break up your pens like that?" asked Rhonda.

Rhonda was one of the few kids in the class who was actually nice to Lenny.

"It makes me feel better," he said.

"But when you do that, you have nothing to write with."

"I know," he said with a sigh. "I can always get one from Mrs. Copper."

"Well, if you say so."

Lenny looked in his pencil box. He only had one pencil pen left. He thought, *Better make sure I don't break this one, or I'll be without a pencil for the rest of the day.*

The next day Lenny searched high and low in his room for extra pencil pens, but there were none to be found. He dared not ask his mother for one because she had just bought him a box of twenty two days ago.

That morning in school, the bully Andrew decided to play a mean trick on Lenny by putting pencil shavings in his chair. Not paying attention, Lenny pulled out his chair and sat down. The shavings were all over his brand new pants.

Mrs. Copper heard his loud shriek and demanded that he see the principal at once. "But look at my brand new pants?" he cried.

"As far as I'm concerned. you did it yourself. Now go to the principal's office at once, young man."

"Yes, Mrs. Copper."

On his way to the principal's office, he ran into Courtney. She told him that she had seen Andrew put the shavings in his chair. She had stepped out of the room for a moment before Mrs. Copper saw him. "You wait right here, and I'll tell Mrs. Copper what happened."

Even though Lenny did many things to annoy Mrs. Copper, she was always fair.

Mrs. Copper even apologized to Lenny. That made him feel great. Later that day they had to change classes for math and science with Mrs. Eddy's class. Mrs. Eddy was about to start going over the assignment for the day when all of the sudden, Lenny's desk fell apart. This time no one saw Andrew take the screws out of his desk. Poor Lenny had no one to come to his defense this time. "Lenny, didn't I tell you the next time you disturbed the class that I would be making a phone call to your mother?"

"Yes, Mrs. Eddy."

"Very well, you may have a seat in John's chair. He's absent today."

Poor Lenny, he was beside himself and exploded with a loud yell and broke his last pencil pen. He had broken so many of Mrs. Eddy's pencils that she refused to give him any more. Poor Lenny, he had no pencil pen for the rest of the day.

That night, at home, Lenny was punished by not being able to watch TV or chat online with his cousin Freddie. His grandmother came over for dinner that night. After dinner, Lenny's mother expressed her concern about Lenny not being able to hold on to his pencils. "I know all about it," she said. "The school called me when they couldn't reach you this afternoon."

"I have just the thing for Lenny."

"Remember when I took that trip to Jamaica with your father two years ago?"

"Yes, Mother, I remember."

"Well, there was this strange little man with a curio shop with all kinds of magical things, so he said. I bought this box of pencil pens in all sorts of bright brilliant colors. He said that they were indestructible and would last a lifetime. I have one with me now. I want Lenny to have it." "Just one, Mother?"

"Yes, that's all he needs."

The next school day Lenny's mother gave him the magical pencil pen. He took it to school. It was a bright green pen that glowed yellow in the dark.

As Lenny sat down in his chair, ready to begin the day, Andrew stepped on his foot. Holding the pen in his hand tightly, about to snap it in two, he heard a funny voice call up to him. "Hey, boy, what you trying to do, break to pieces in half?"

Lenny giggled to himself. "You can talk!"

"Of course, I can, can't you?"

"Lenny, what are you doing?"

"Nothing, Mrs. Copper."

At recess, Lenny found a quiet corner in the playground to talk to his new friend. It was a strange thing to see. He wondered if he should share this with Courtney. She was his best friend. "Can anyone else hear you besides me?"

"Only if you want them to, boy."

"How come you talk so funny?"

"I'm from a long, long way from here boy. Me from Jamaica. De Island of beautiful white sandy beaches and de bluest skies you ever did see, boy."

"Look!" cried Lenny. "Your top turned into a straw hat."

"Oh, me hat goes wherever me goes."

After school, they would frolic in the park, lying in the deep green grass. Lenny would tell the pencil pen all about his troubles. "You know what you need, boy?"

"No, what do I need?"

"You need some anger management. That's what you need."

"Why do I need that when everybody's always picking on me?"

"Well, now I'll tell you why. It's because you show them too much how bad they hurt your feelings. Now take me. I bend and shake, and you can't make me cry." He goes into a song and dance. "No matter what you do, you can't make me. No matter what you do can't make me. You can't bend me or break me. So why don't you give up this fight? I say again, no matter what you do, you can't bend or break me, so why don't you give up the fight?"

"So what you're saying is that I shouldn't let them upset me?"

"Right! That's it, boy. You never let them know how mad you are. If they think what they're doing isn't upsetting you, then they won't bothers you no more."

"That's all I have to do?"

"That's right, boy."

"That's going to be hard for me, especially with Andrew around."

"Well, that's the only way, boy. Now you practice with me."

Lenny bent and shook with all his might, still the pencil pen would not break.

The next day at school, Andrew continued to make life miserable for Lenny. This time he poured the pencil shaving on top of Lenny's head while Mrs. Copper wasn't looking. Some of the children began to laugh. "All right," Mrs. Copper said to the class. "That wasn't a nice thing to do to whomever did that. I never realized how many bratlings I had in my class before. I think you all owe Lenny an apology."

In unison, they all said, "We're sorry, Lenny."

Lenny felt great. He had never had the whole class apologize for anything. He learned by ignoring someone, that it takes all the pleasure out of their fun.

What everyone didn't see was that Lenny kept bending his pencil pen to keep from getting mad and reacting to Andrew's negativity. Lenny finally learned that no one, not even Andrew, likes to be ignored.

The End.

ACTIVITY ZONE

1. What do you think of the story
   "Lenny and the Pencil Pen"?

ACTIVITY ZONE

2. Do you have a best friend whom you cherish?
Please *draw* your best friend and what you like to do.

ACTIVITY ZONE

3. What do you like to do at school?

A SURPRISE PARTY FOR MRS. COPPER

About the Cat Hiding in the Drier

It was just about to be dismissal time at Unity Rainbow Charter School. Rhonda, Courtney, and Babs were huddled in a corner of the hall, chattering away regarding a secret. Tiny Tina Terra was lurking about as usual, trying to find out about the secret. As Babs was fixing her hair, looking in the mirror, she spotted Tiny Tina Terra peeking around the corner.

She slammed her locker door. "Girls, terror alert, terror alert!"

"I know you're behind that wall," said Rhonda.

"Come out, Tina Terra, we know you're there," said Courtney.

"What do you want anyway?" said Babs.

"I know you guys are up to something, and unless you tell me, I'll tell Ms. Eddy that you were the ones who put chocolate pudding in her Pepsi."

"You wouldn't dare," said Rhonda. "Besides, it was an accident."

"Not the way I'm going to tell it." Tiny Tina Terra smirked.

Babs chimed in, "But it was an accident. We were giving out the pudding cups when one was open from the bottom, and it fell into her glass of soda."

"Sure, you've convinced me, but I don't think Ms. Eddy will see it that way."

"Okay, Tina, you've got us over a barrel, but you can't tell anyone else about the secret."

"Okay, I won't."

Babs started to tell her about the surprise birthday party for Mrs. Copper. "Ms. Eddy is going to help us make the arrangements."

Just then Spring Jones walked by. "Hey, what's up?"

Tiny Tina Terra started pushing her away, shouting, "It's none of your business!"

"Let go of me before I squash you like a bug," said Spring.

"Do we have to tell her?" cried Tiny Tina Terra.

"I think it'll be all right," said Rhonda.

Tiny Tina Terra fouled her arms across her chest and began seething as usual.

"Okay, here's the plan," Rhonda began.

Everyone was excited, all except Tiny Tina Terra. "I'll get my mom to bake the cake," said Babs.

"I'll get my mom to make the lady finger sandwiches," said Rhonda.

"I'll take care of the punch," said Courtney.

"I'll bring the party favors and ice cream," said Spring. "What's she going to bring?" asked Spring, pointing toward Tiny Tina Terra.

"She's going to bring herself and a promise to keep her mouth shut," said Rhonda with her fist balled up at Tiny Tina Terra.

"I know what we can use terror for," said Babs. "We can get her to find out what Mrs. Copper's favorite color is!" She turned to Tina. "Terror–"

"First of all, stop calling me terror, it's Terra."

"Okay, fair enough."

They all agreed to call her Tina Terra.

All of a sudden, Benny shows up.

"What are you guys talking about?"

"Mrs. Copper's birthday party."

"No!" shouted Tiny Tina Terra. "It's already too many people finding out about the party."

"She has a point," said Courtney. "Maybe we better not let anyone else in on it."

"All right. Benny, since you know about the party, I guess we have to let you in on it."

"Good, now what do I do?" asked Benny.

"Nothing," said Rhonda. "Simply nothing."

"But that means I can't help out."

"Oh, believe me, Benny, that's help enough," said Courtney.

"I don't get it," said Benny.

"That's the beauty of it, you don't," said Courtney.

The bell had rang, it was time for everyone to leave school. The next school day Tiny Tina Terra was asking Mrs. Copper all kinds of questions. "You know, Mrs. Copper, my mother has that same color sweater that you're wearing. Is green your favorite color?" Before Mrs. Copper could answer, Tina went on and on. "Or maybe pink, pink would look very nice on you. No, instead, maybe baby blue or orange, no, no, purple."

"Tina!" shouted Courtney, gritting her teeth. "You're asking too many questions, she might get the right idea," she said, pulling her to the side. "You're going to ruin the surprise."

"Oh," said Tina. "I guess I got too excited. I be more careful from now on."

Just then, a student from Ms. Eddy's class came in with a note.

Mrs. Copper reads the note, "Ms. Eddy would like for the following students to come to her class to go over the science project: Rhonda, Courtney, Spring, Benny, Babs, and"–with her eyes opening wide–"and Tina Terra."

When they arrived, Ms. Eddy told them it's not much time because the party is for the next day. The next morning Mrs. Copper is feeling a little sad because her Tabby, the family cat, had gotten frightened by the thunderstorm the night before. Ms. Eddy tried to cheer her up, but nothing seemed to work.

That afternoon the children came in with the surprise party. Mrs. Copper forced a big smile. Just then, Mr. Copper called her on the phone to say that the cat had not ran away at all. She was behind the clothes drier the whole time.

"I feel much, much better now," said Mrs. Copper.

All the children sang "Happy Birthday." Mrs. Copper grabbed Tiny Tina Terra and said, "Happy birthday to you!"

It wasn't Mrs. Copper's birthday after all. The party was for Tiny Tina Terra. "We had to keep you busy so that you wouldn't know about our surprise party for you," said Rhonda.

"You do seem to get into things," said Courtney.

Tiny Tina Terra, for once, was speechless. She could only beam.

ACTIVITY ZONE

1. Do you have a pet? Describe how you feel about having a pet.

ACTIVITY ZONE

2. Please color the cat.

ACTIVITY ZONE

3. What would you do if you have a pet?

BRATLINGS GO FOR THE GOLD

It's the big day for Unity Rainbow Charter School's soccer and softball events, and the Bratlings are going up against the reigning champs the Royal Lions. Their only hope is that their best softball player Boogs can beat the Royal Lions' best player Richie Santiago. Mickey warns Boogs to watch out for Richie's fast ball. "Now remember what I said, Bogs, watch out for his fast ball. He's a mean right-hander."

As far as Boogs being the best player, Candy felt she was just as good as or better than any boy on the team. She challenges Mr. Cherry on why she can't compete against the boys. "Ever hear of Monica Jackson?" she asked.

Mr. Cherry concedes and puts her on the team.

Mickey protests the inclusion of girls being on the team. "Girls only slow up the paste of the game. They can't run as fast as the boys or hit as hard as the boys."

Mr. Cherry reminds Mickey that we're in the twenty-first century and that girls and women can pretty much do as well as men and boys. "If you say so, Mr. Cherry, but I still think you're making a big mistake."

Since there's a big hole in the school's budget, many of the staff have taken on other positions to prevent massive layoffs. Mr. Cherry is crossing guard/recreation manager. Westley agrees with Mr. Cherry and insists that they must keep an open mind about including girls on the team. "It's okay, Mick, I've seen hear play in a few games with some of the neighborhoods guys, and she's pretty good."

"Yeah, fine and dandy, but we're talking about Richie Santiago."

"Please, Mr. Cherry, this is not the time for political correctness," he cries.

Mr. Cherry tells Mickey that he's sticking to his guns. "I understand your concern about going up against the best player in the school. However, this is a democracy we live in, and that means everyone gets a chance to show what he or she can do. It's a sense of fair play, something many people in the grown-up world doesn't practice enough of."

"All right, I get the message loud and clear."

The school's principal, Mr. Bottoms, announced over the PA system, "First up will be our soccer team. The first team to score five goals will be the winner."

The players take their place on the field. The teams are all female. There are the Bratlings from Mrs. Copper's class, next the Royal Lionesses from Ms. Eddy's class, and finally, the Wildcats from Mrs. Carter's class. The girls are all strategically spread throughout the field. Babs takes the first kick. However, Big Strodder proves to be more than she can handle. Strodder blocks the net. Next up is Carmen Menedez from Mrs. Carter's class. And Strodder gives a nice block of the net. Now it's the turn of the Royal Lionesses. Strodder takes the first kick, the ball flies over the opposing team's heads. She does a second and again and again. She does it winning five in a row. The winners are the Royal Lionesses. Now comes the game the whole school's been waiting. The Wildcats didn't make the grade to be in the playoffs. It's now just the two best teams: the Bratlings and the Royal Lions.

First up is Jimmy Smith of the Royal Lions. Boogs is the pitcher. He winds up and throws a fast ball. Jimmy hits it clean out of the field, giving his team a home run. Next up to pitch is Candy. She throws a fast fast ball. Jimmy swings with all his might but misses the ball. He digs his heels in deeper for more support but still unable to hit the

ball. Each player who takes the bat seems unable to outdo Candy's fast balls. Finally, it's Richie Santiago's turn to pitch.

This is the moment everyone was waiting for. Richie has been the champ for the past three years. No one's ever beaten him ever. He takes his place up on the mound. Boogs is sweating bullets before he even takes a swing. Richie throws his famous fast ball. It skits past the right side of Boogs. He could almost feel the burn from the ball. He strikes Boogs out. Next, it's Lenny's turn to bat; he too is struck out. Then comes Mickey, he puts up a good fight but is still no match for Richie.

Finally, it's Candy's turn at the mound, and Richie is at the bat. She throws her fast ball. Richie misses. She throws another and another until he's struck out. He's so exhausted from hitting Candy's fast balls that he's completely blown away when it's Boogs turn to pitch again. Boogs lifts his left leg and throws his power ball with all his might. Richie swings but misses the ball.

Richie stares Boogs down with his steely green eyes. Boogs isn't fazed, it keeps up the pace with his power balls. Mr. Cherry, who's also the umpire, shouts, "Strike three! You're out!"

The Bratlings win the gold cup. Mickey walks over to Candy and admits he was wrong. He offers her a handshake.

"You still think girls can't cut the mustard?"

"Nah, you're just one of the guys now."

He and Lenny help the others on the team lift Candy and Boogs on their shoulders, carrying them off the field to victory and fries and a milkshake, compliments of Mr. Cherry.

The End

ACTIVITY ZONE

1. What do you like to do at school?

ACTIVITY ZONE

COLORING TIME

ACTIVITY ZONE

2. Do you like to go to school?

THE MYSTERY OF NURSE BAND-AID

On a cold windy, rainy day, the kids in Mrs. Copper's class were looking for excitement to chase away the boredom. Westley, who suffered from frequent nosebleeds, was about to have one. He tried to get Mrs. Copper's attention, to ask if he could go to the nurse's office. She was busy teaching the class their new spelling words and didn't hear him.

"What's wrong?" Mickey whispered to him.

"My nose is starting to bleed. I think I need to go and see the nurse."

There was a new nurse at the school, but already, the news was going around that she killed a kid. "No!" Shouted Mickey.

"Is there a problem, young man?" asked Mrs. Copper.

"No, there's no problem, Mrs. Copper," Mickey replied.

Leaning closer to Westley, he told him of the urban legend about the nurse who had only been at the school for six months. "Didn't you hear about her?"

"No," Westley said.

"She killed a kid at her old school, and they transferred her here because they couldn't prove it."

Westley chuckled. "Come on, you're lying!"

Just then, Tiny Tina Terra joined in the conversation. "He's right. They called her Nurse Band-Aid."

"I don't believe it." Westley still wasn't convinced.

Just then, Mrs. Copper looked away from the white board. "I see I'm going to have to do some seat changes if the talking among you three keeps up."

"Wait, I think the bleeding has stopped," said Westley.

"Good," said Mickey.

At recess, Lenny told Westley the story about the boy who went missing from the other school. He told of how all the kids at school would wait 'til they got home to tell their parents if they were sick or in need of a doctor.

"The way I heard it, it was about a year ago," Lenny starts off. "The boy had a splinter in his palm from the old grab bars in the gym. He went to see Nurse Band-Aid. She supposedly gave him this stuff to drink to take away the pain."

Babs overheard him and said, "How does drinking something take away the pain from a splinter?"

"You take the splinter out, and it's done with."

"You want to hear the story or not?"

"*Oh*, have it your way."

Clearing his throat, ah hum, Lenny continues with the story.

"Anyway, she gave him this thick white milky stuff, and the kid started going into convulsions. They said his eyes started to bulge, and you could see the red veins swelling up in them. The stuff started coming out of his nose, and he started to turn blue and purple, and I can't go on."

"No, don't stop now," said Mickey.

"I know," said Tiny Tina Terra. "My cousin went to that school, and he said the boy's head exploded."

"Yeah, that's right," said Lenny.

"Then what happened?" asked Babs.

"They said the principal went into the office and helped her sneak the body out with the recycling. They told the recycling guy on the truck that it was a dummy they used in the first-aid class."

"Lenny, I still think you're making this all up," said Babs. "Ms. Marshell is a very nice person."

"How would you know?" asked Lenny.

"Well, Courtney went to see her last week for a scraped knee, and she was very kind and gentle. *Oh*, FYI, she knows about the name Nurse Band-Aid. She likes it and doesn't mind it at all. By the way, Westley, your nose is starting to bleed again. Go and see Ms. Marshell."

Westley took her advice and went to see the nurse.

"Boy, what a killjoy you are, Babs," said Lenny.

Westley nervously entered the nurse's office. A pretty and cheerful Ms. Marshell greeted him. "Hi, I see you have a pretty nasty nosebleed there. Let me see what I can do to take away the pain."

She smelled of sweet flowers in a summer breeze, and her hands were cool and soft to the touch. She placed a cold towel to the bridge of his nose to stop the flow of blood. Soon, within minutes, he felt better. He smiled and said, "Thank you," almost about to say the name they called her.

"You're welcome. Just call me Nurse Band-Aid." She winked.

Westley laughed a nervous laugh and went on his way.

The End.

ACTIVITY ZONE

1. Have you ever had a time when you were injured?

ACTIVITY ZONE

2. How did it feel?

ACTIVITY ZONE

3. What is your dream job?

Printed in the United States
by Baker & Taylor Publisher Services